Nobody has a name like Jesus O'Flynn. And it's true Jesus was not his name.

But Mr. Charisman called him Jesus because that is what O'Flynn had said the first time he glimpsed the dimensions of the creature who called himself, idiotically, Mr. Charisman. Mr. Charisman was a gigantic excrescence with many moving mouths that argued with one another, that snapped and drooled over O'Flynn in a manner altogether disgusting.

But if Mr. Charisman was a nightmare, what he wanted O'Flynn to do was utter madness.

On the other hand, even utter madness can look sane when one has a time bomb planted in one's body . . .

Other Titles by Brian N. Ball

TIMEPIECE

Also Available from Ballantine Books

A Ballantine Books Original Publication

TIMEPIVOT

by Brian N. Ball

BALLANTINE BOOKS • NEW YORK
An Intext Publisher

BALLANTINE BOOKS, INC.
101 Fifth Avenue, New York, N.Y. 10003

FOR TOM KAISER

Prologue

Time drifted onto the ruin of the Galactic Federation. The centuries rolled over the wars of the first part of the new millennium, laying their patina of forgetfulness over the adventures of the survivors of the expedition to the Forever Planet. Only in the memory banks of lost and ruined computers was there a record of the writhing piece of time, hung in its weird universe, poised in a matrix of *forevers,* which had waited eons to release its makers from their imprisonment on a planet which was their plaything, workshop, laboratory and engine.

No one returned to the planet.

Not of his own volition.

Its gross asymmetry still remained, however. The encapsulated piece of time which had served to propel the planet's slaves—and then masters once more—back into their own universe was not diminished in power. The asymmetry in space and time remained.

And the ships which strayed out into the gulfs of the dimensions beyond the Galaxy, across the black pits of emptiness in search of a fixed point of reference to guide them back to the safety of the charted flows of space-time?

Some returned, unscathed.

But an occasional unfortunate crew came into contact with the terrifying enigma—the frozen *function* of space-time—which came to be called the Timepivot.

Of those that were lost, a few found a place in legend.

Chapter 1

O'Flynn jerked hard on the crowbar. A thin chunk of rock flew upward under the impetus of the steel in his muscular arms. He turned to the blasting crew and signaled for the cumbersome drills to be brought forward. For the thousandth time he tried to mop sweat from his dull-green visor. He stopped the action before it was complete; this jagged satellite had no atmosphere, and Operation Plutarch could not afford the frills of an artificial envelope of air on a remote moon in a tiny system out on the rim of the Galaxy. The sweat dried as the efficient sensors in his air pack detected an excess of moisture.

"Take it here. Secondary charges spread at three-meter radials."

"Will do, O'Flynn."

There was more than a little of muted admiration in the ready acceptance of his instructions, but O'Flynn was not aware of it; his mind was entirely on the coming shock wave which would neatly level another of the sharp-edged cliffs, leaving nothing but a few heaps of rubble for the giant crushers to grind into a heavy, compacted powder. There was always a sense of fulfillment in the chopping down of the last major ridge on the last mountain chain of a planet; it was the taming of another wild and disordered landscape, so that the vision of Plutarch could become reality. Here, riding its unliving path around a dying sun, the satellite would become one more of the chains of symmetrical spheres which, mirror-like, would beam a true reflection of light to the blackness beyond the Galaxy.

The charges were quickly in place. The three others in his team were humping the drills down to the bug below; O'Flynn caught a glimpse of Karanja's grin, and a smile broke out onto his own face. It was a good team, one of the best: Karanja; Preston, who thought he might be a reincarnation of the monk Rasputin; and Lingelbach, the immense, slow-moving drill-handler. O'Flynn held his hand out in the gesture that meant "Retire." They were used to his taciturnity at the end of a big project, so they said nothing. They would talk later, when the job was done. Then the singing would begin, and soon Lingelbach would be bellowing for cold beer, Karanja calling for the project director to celebrate the end of their work in the system, while Preston dressed himself ritually in the black robes of a long-dead seer from the beginnings of time.

O'Flynn caught the mood of his team from their lighthearted leaps down the ridge; he returned from his contemplation of a score of neat, huge reshapings of the crusts of a dozen moons like this. He waved to the team, shaking a fist at Lingelbach, who coiled the big cables around his shoulders as if they were so much twine, and who tossed the massive drill ahead like a javelin.

"He's just playful," called Karanja. "Cut it out, will you!" He yelped into the echoing suit as Lingelbach effortlessly tossed him across a fissure which ran for miles into the depths of the planet. Lingelbach burst into song, the march which never failed to send a shaking of pride through O'Flynn. But he ordered Lingelbach to keep off the air, nevertheless.

"And use the bridge!"

Karanja was about to jump back over the fissure just as a purplish splash of dust jetted upward from it. Seeing it, Karanja crossed by the temporary bridge.

O'Flynn looked down into the fissure, quietly satisfied with his plan. The ridge high above him would topple to fill it, the gases which boiled out intermittently would be plugged down. Then the crushers could smooth out what was left. He felt again the prickling at the back of his neck which always accompanied the fierce swellings of pride that came when he remembered the responsibilities he carried, and the mighty nature

4

of the operation. He grinned. Lingelbach was humming the order's march.

The charges had been set perfectly. It was a textbook explosion. The ridge heaved itself upward and outward. It hung, black and cragged against a violet horizon, and then it poured out in an almost liquid flow into the valleys below.

O'Flynn watched the completion of this phase of Operation Plutarch. He was about to tell Karanja to call up the crushers when a small sliver of quartzite rolled to a stop in front of him.

"Do we call them down?" asked Karanja. He was impatient to be away.

"Just a minute."

It wasn't quartzite, though it was embedded in solid rock. It wasn't rock of any kind; the thing he had picked up couldn't have come from the ridge at all. It was totally out of place in this silent waste of broken rock and heavy dust.

Aloud, O'Flynn said, "What's a high-temperature thermal calibrator doing here?"

Chapter 2

The shimmering blip that was the supply base, equipment store and recreation center for the blasting crews and their more humble colleagues, the moonscape laborers, was in sight. Karanja plunged ahead with a bellow of delight; the job was over. In a couple of days, new orders would come from Galactic Center. The blip would grow tentacles of power waves and begin the long haul to the outskirts of the regular shipping lanes, where it would wait for one of the big hyperspace vessels. Then, hitched to the bulk of the liner, it would surge through the interstices of space and time until it was shrugged off to decelerate into a credible framework of celestial bodies, where ordinary things like suns wheeled through the cobwebs of the systems, and where more dead moons waited to be shaped into gleaming regularity. But until the orders arrived, the team would go catatonic.

Lingelbach would do it with drugged visions, in which his strength would multiply a hundredfold. He would crush boulders in fists of iron and hug armored, meteorproof drilling rigs against his chest, to wrinkle them in ponderous, powerful movements. He was a man to keep clear of, for he could flick the life from an ordinary human frame with a casual stroke of his arm. Preston, too, was dangerous in the days of waiting. He had absorbed every jot of knowledge to survive the cataclysm of Blow-up; the result of his dream-injected state was an urge to perform grotesque rituals with whatever material at hand. He had sacrificed a visiting inspector on one notable occasion, to the delight of the admiring crusher team. Galactic Center had been understanding. Visitors were warned of the behavior of the pioneers who worked on Operation Plutarch. Only Karanja had gentle impulses during the privileged period. He used an archaic form of

6

release, a concoction which was worshipped in the days of the early spacemen. It came to the supply base in bottles. And that was how Karanja drank it; by the bottle.

O'Flynn found himself unexcited by the prospect of his own approaching bout of conditioned release. Usually he took an excursion into the total experience simulators, the Totex Globes; he had been O'Flynn the sense-swimmer, O'Flynn the conqueror of the Silurians, whoever they were, and—twice—O'Flynn, the strongest blade on Vega. And more. He looked at the blip which was his home.

"Now, how could a sensor and calibrator for liquid rock get into a three-hundred-million-year-old Archean stratum?"

"Give it up!" called Karanja, and O'Flynn realized he had been talking aloud. "We're through here, and what an honor it's been to work with the immaculate O'Flynn once more. Man, the way you lifted that last ridge clean into the valleys—the touch of genius, O'Flynn!"

"You were good, O'Flynn," joined in Lingelbach.

"If it worries you, call Base."

Preston wanted a share of no man's troubles at this moment. He was savoring the delirium of his impending descent into fantasy. O'Flynn could almost smell the sickly incense the dark man would use. That, and the raw stink of blood.

"Call Base?"

They were still a few minutes walk away. And after they reached the blip they would have to stow the equipment and send their suits to the decontamination squad. It would be a simple matter for Base to find the answer to the puzzle of the highly expensive calibrator which was stuck so firmly into the sliver of age-old rock ripped from Satellite 13A/B7/5. It shouldn't, couldn't be there. And yet it was.

"This is O'Flynn. Keep out of it, you guys," he motioned to the team—Karanja grinning, Preston uninterested, Lingelbach barely understanding.

"We have you, O'Flynn. Give."

"So we finished the ridge. You can send the boys in when you wish. . ."

"Look behind you."

The immense machines rolled ghostlike over the smashed satellite. Somewhere within the complex of force-shields and flailing mechanisms of each of them sat a rider who directed the program filed by Base. The machines plunged on in line, the superfluous directors contentedly feeding in the contour plans. O'Flynn could never fail to be impressed by the sheer bulk of the crushers.

"I see them."

"The problem?"

O'Flynn wondered whose voice the robot control used. Or was it an artificial mixture of sounds and intonation?

"Nothing much. But check it out, will you? I found what looks like—is—a meter for liquid rock temperatures in the ridge."

"Your own equipment?"

"It couldn't be. I've never brought ours from Base. No need to. In any case, this is a real precision job."

"Your team? Would any one of them carry it?"

"No." The team? Karanja, Lingelbach or Preston leave any item of equipment behind!

"You were right to report this."

"I wouldn't have troubled, but it was the age of the rock around it!"

"Describe it."

O'Flynn took the glistening rock and gave a geologist's concise description. Any member of his team could have done so.

"Here we come!" put in Karanja, disregarding O'Flynn's instructions to stay off the air. "They've found a new brand for me—brewed with soil-grown malt barley!"

"Remain where you are."

O'Flynn and his team were still plunging forward against the oddly heavy gravity of the small satellite. Lingelbach, slowest of understanding, was the first to stop.

"Here?"

"Stay here!"

"Why?"

Lingelbach was puzzled, Karanja disappointed, and Preston quarrelsome about the inexplicable order.

The team moved closer together, for a mystery had taken shape. Base had never seemed so far away, even though the shining blip was only a mile distant. When they had been moving toward it, the desolation of the moonscape had been a factor in their existence; it was the backcloth of their working life. Now the black and gray scree, with the occasional gleam of bright ore, began to take on a new meaning for them.

Linglebach, unperceptive and slow, spoke for them all when he said, "I never felt cold like this."

O'Flynn looked down at the tiny anachronistic thing set so securely in ancient rock. Preston reached out a hand for it. His thin face glowered down at O'Flynn.

"Is this why?"

"That's it!" Karanja shouted. "It must be. Is it, O'Flynn? Something to do with the operation here? Has it fouled up the contours plan?"

O'Flynn held his gauntlet with the rock-embedded meter. He was never to know what Preston made of the thing, for Base called at that moment.

"O'Flynn!"

O'Flynn paused. There was a curt peremptoriness about the voice that compelled instant attention. The others stiffened, alert and obedient. The empty landscape was forgotten; they were O'Flynn's team, the best in the business.

He was finding it difficult to reply to the robot voice. The muscles of his throat had unaccountably stiffened; his gaze was fixed on the rock-cased instrument he was still holding out to Preston.

"O'Flynn! Report!"

"Yes. You've found who lost it?"

"You are ordered to disconnect your communicator."

Three faces registered degrees of shock and incredulity, Lingelbach's slowest of all. Except O'Flynn's. Even as the big man's eyes widened, he could feel the symptoms of shock invading his system, finding expression at last in the sag of his jaw and the stretching of the muscles around his eyes.

His fingers were already on the emergency cut-out which would sever connections between himself, his team and Base.

"Report, O'Flynn! Do you understand?"

"Disconnect. Yes." His fingers refused to obey. "It must be faulty. It's contaminated. That's why, isn't it?"

"Obey."

O'Flynn, master of a difficult trade, product of a system he could never understand, conditioned since birth to the acceptance of robot control, still hesitated. In its way, it was a failure of the system, shown to be so by the response of the three watchers. Their hands twitched, unconsciously urging O'Flynn's own hands into motion. Their heads nodded in unison within the bulky plastic domes they wore, agreeing with O'Flynn's small movements, willing him to comply with Base's strange but undeniable command.

"Yes."

O'Flynn turned away from his men and aimed a finger at the button. He jabbed solidly at a spot an inch away from it. He could not have said what prompted him to ignore the command. The stiffening of the hairs on his neck could have told him something, but didn't, any more than the slight forward stretching of the muscles behind and below his ears. The sudden tremendous increase in his blood circulation did, however, let him know that he was under stress. As soon as the symptoms of fear and readiness to confront danger occurred, he had rationalized his decision; he had not disobeyed in any spirit of deliberate insubordination. No. Base had forgotten that he was responsible for the team. Without him, they might fail to complete the schedule set down for the completion of the task; they might not service the drills, for instance. Lingelbach might leave his pack of explosives in the decontamination chambers. Karanja was sure to forget to change the seismographic soundings.

O'Flynn grinned at the team.

"What do you suppose—" began Karanja in a shocked whisper.

O'Flynn made the sign that signified "Don't worry." The others nodded back at him, miming encouragement.

Lingelbach unshipped his pack, clearly with the intention of reassuring O'Flynn. As he made the "Leave it to me" sign, Base came on once more.

"O'Flynn is no longer your squad commander."

The three men began to talk. They stared at one another, looking away from O'Flynn. Alert to their embarrassed attempts to cover their confusion, O'Flynn restored a semblance of his normal good-humored expression. Base was talking again.

"O'Flynn has broken the Code."

He felt cold despair engulfing him. The members of Operation Plutarch were a dedicated, specialized and honored body; their rules permitted no failures, no questioning of operation commanders, no resignations and, particularly, no infringements of the Code. Even through his fear, he contrived to remain outwardly calm. He raised a hand to Lingelbach. "Sure," his action said. "I trust you, Lingelbach."

The big face was that of a stranger. Preston's thin face regarded him with an air of clinical loathing; Karanja had turned away. Sickly gripings clutched at O'Flynn's insides. Karanja too?

"O'Flynn has been sentenced."

It was a robot voice. No human voice could have remained so unchanged through the grim message. Preston advanced half a pace toward O'Flynn. In that moment, O'Flynn shed his twenty-five years of preparation for service with the operation. He became animal.

Base had been in touch with Galactic Control, probably at Sector level; so one part of his mind said, that which was still in touch with the larger situation. Base would carry out sentence, just as it always did, quickly and remorselessly, with whatever means were at hand; so another part of his mind told him, the part which watched Preston, since Preston was the immediate danger.

"Kill him."

Chapter 3

Preston's face was a mask of incredulous delight. He was the danger. The other two, one slow, the other still held by the old loyalties, had made no move. In one quick movement, O'Flynn held out the shard of rock, Preston automatically reached for it.

Without hesitation O'Flynn thrust stiff-armed at the plastic helmet. The sharp point burst through. Air rushed to expand in the vacuum, to be followed by a spurting of blood. O'Flynn saw death coming into Preston's remaining eye, the eye fixed on the cause of O'Flynn's condemnation and his own killing.

"Firing!"

O'Flynn bellowed the word of warning. Old habits and years of training threw Lingelbach and Karanja sideways and downward, away from danger; they had moved like this a thousand times in practice. And once in earnest, on a satellite bigger than this, when a geological fault had revealed itself as the pattern of charges went up ahead of time. Only the word of warning yelled by O'Flynn had saved them. This time it might save O'Flynn.

For how long?

O'Flynn surged away from the two men, sparing a second or two to throw off his pack; without thought he grabbed Lingelbach's heavier load.

"O'Flynn is Outcast! Kill on sight! All units report now!"

Base began to issue individual commands. The three teams resting were to join the hunt; all operations were to stop; O'Flynn was the first priority. Pounding heart furnishing strength to slow-seeming limbs, eyes bulging with effort, despair urging him to halt and die at the hands of his men, O'Flynn could still think. It was the

12

thermal meter. The anachronism. The thing that had impossibly grown into rock which had once been an ooze of mud in some remote past. Finding it was important enough to mean his death. And his own men would kill him.

Would they?

O'Flynn looked over his shoulder.

What he saw brought a strangled scream to his throat. Karanja was outpacing Lingelbach; both were almost on him, even though he had always prided himself on his athletic ability. He moved faster. Then something clicked into place: they had discarded their packs.

Why had he scooped up that heavy load of explosives? Because Lingelbach might leave them lying about a forbidden area? Because the big man might forget to disarm the small nuclear charges before he put them into store? It couldn't be. He could trust Lingelbach. O'Flynn began to curse his failing limbs, to curse his confused thoughts, to curse bleakly and bitterly his damn curiosity. He could trust—there was no doubt about it. But loyalty was a matter of degree; at the highest level, it held strongest. They would kill him.

He did scream when he saw the direction of his flight.

He was heading for Base.

And Base had ordered the crushers to join the hunt. In a ring, Base said coldly. In a ring around Base. And then move in, obliterating everything.

O'Flynn could sense the ground trembling under the sharp impact of the immense machines as they changed direction in unison. Soon they would ring poor worn-out, lumbering, pack-impeded, condemned, almost hopeless O'Flynn.

He stopped. Turned. Measured distances.

"I'll wait," he called.

His voice was equable, friendly—the man who had helped get the team top ratings in the Sector. Incredibly, the other two slowed.

"It's orders, O'Flynn." Karanja was gasping.

"Orders." Lingelbach sounded sorry. His sorrow

13

would not stop the ponderous lunge to O'Flynn's head.

"All right. I know."

O'Flynn had the pack off. He sat on it, a tired man waiting for the inevitable; it seemed he had accepted his sentence.

With the cunning of a trapped animal, O'Flynn judged the range perfectly. His hand slipped into the pack, coming out fluidly with a small, armed charge. Three deft movements transformed it into an impact bomb, a powerful thrust sent it winging over the rock and dust. O'Flynn slipped behind the pack to avoid the heat generated by the impact. He did not trouble to watch the two men staggering about, their suits penetrated and their limbs and bodies scorched.

He had a few minutes before the teams at Base could be ready to emerge; perhaps enough time to enter the outer lock before the crushers rolled over the bodies of his team, all the while diminishing the perimeter of his zone of action.

"O'Flynn is dead," he gasped. He staggered on, hoping for a few minutes of indecision on the part of Base control.

"Report."

"Karanja!" he gasped. His legs were iron bars, his body a mountain of lead ore. Two minutes to Base. Less if he ran.

"Lingelbach! Preston! Report!"

"Injured," said O'Flynn. "Both injured. Send the emergency bug!"

Half a minute, if he could keep up this pace. He tore off the belt that housed his personal kit of tools; irreplaceable, he thought sadly. Like the life he had left behind the moment he had turned over the embedded meter. Life? O'Flynn muttered it aloud. "Life?"

"Report!" commanded the iron voice.

"Hurt . . . O'Flynn dead . . . blasted us . . . wounded."

Almost there. The smooth evenness of Base reared above him. Suddenly the equipment bay lay open and out of it came the little emergency bug with its glittering array of rescue gear sparkling in the dying violet light.

14

O'Flynn watched it pass, one more obstacle removed. The way into the lock was clear.

There were perhaps three hundred personnel in the honeycombed layers of Base; three hundred alert enemies impelled to his killing by the flat, metallic, almost disinterested robot which interpreted the policy of Sector Control, which again and in its turn deferred to the central authority at Galactic Control. O'Flynn had a moment of insight into the hidden immensity of his task: survival, when condemned by those—men? robots?—who were, or had been, his masters.

"Has O'Flynn's body been located?" demanded Base Control.

O'Flynn, alive, trembling, nerves keyed, dejectedly afraid, bitterly aggressive, but still hoping that the nightmare of his condemnation would suddenly evaporate—O'Flynn, a middle-sized powerful figure in the suit which he had no time to discard, plunged into the normal gravity of the space beyond the lock. He had no knowledge of how he might overcome his enemies, the three hundred humans and the one deadly robot, but he knew what he must do if he was to remain alive long enough to convince Sector Control, or even Galactic Center itself that he, O'Flynn, was no danger: he had to kill, kill again and again, somehow contrive the mass slaughter of his human enemies, and the destruction of the thing at the center of Base.

This and more passed through O'Flynn's mind in the few seconds it took him to pass through the cavern which housed the ranks of unused machinery; he was counting the seconds still remaining before the three teams could be ready to begin the hunt. He discarded the thought of his coming confrontation with the robot controller even before it took shape; the immediate dangers were his own kind.

A shrill clamor bounced around his helmet and through the bones of his skull. The Disaster siren. It rose to a screaming crescendo, noise penetrating from the outside as well as from his own communicator. The force of the noise impelled him forward in a shambling

15

run; panic, fear and hate mingled to give a numbed impetus to his now undirected movements.

"O'Flynn is not dead! O'Flynn is loose here at Base! Kill on sight!"

The wide entrance lock behind him was sealed. Ahead, a burst of light showed him that someone had opened the inner locks. The noise was gone, though its echoes still shouted in his ears.

O'Flynn burst among the dozen or so maintenance men with a roar of anguish. Instinct drove him forward, some remnant of training making him flick on the power supply to his harness so that he now swept men into shocked, ruined heaps of blood and smashed bone with the same force which enabled men of his calling to manhandle the great drills up soaring cliffs. Behind them were the half-prepared men who so recently had been his colleagues in an honored profession.

"Report!" the metallic voice commanded. "Where is O'Flynn?"

Some unseen watcher tersely told of O'Flynn's berserk entry; it ended on a sob as O'Flynn again launched himself forward.

He found himself gasping their names: Lingelbach, Karanja—no, they were dead; cold and black-faced with the dying violet light glimmering on them. He killed other friends now with a savage pity.

"O'Flynn! O'Flynn!" The robot was worried.

"Coming!"

But where? And what could he *do?*

"Where *is* O'Flynn?"

"Loose in the Screening Area."

There was resignation in the unseen watcher's voice; it described horror and violence almost apathetically.

"O'Flynn must be killed! O'Flynn endangers the whole operation! Sector Control advises immediate execution. Where is O'Flynn?" It was a rhetorical question. "O'Flynn is in the Administrative Area. O'Flynn must die. Humans cannot kill him." There was a solution, the metallic voice implied. "Disaster in Base Seven," it said. "Operational orders provide for the failure of human personnel."

16

O'Flynn looked around the rooms he had never seen before. Men had cowered at his approach, tumbling over one another to avoid his fear-impelled circuit of death; he no longer troubled to lunge at them. His own fear had triggered off a wild, manic terror among them.

Then he noticed the stillness around him.

His enemies collapsed, one by one. As if at some command, they slid to the floor and remained there in glazed astonishment.

"Dead?" whispered O'Flynn.

"O'Flynn is dead," said the robot. "All human personnel at Base are dead. New humans must be sent."

Dead? O'Flynn went from room to room.

Corpses stared at the dust on his boots.

He propped himself against a desk. Its owner moved away from him, unbalanced by the slight impact of his heavy-suited body. O'Flynn watched the dead man descend to join the others. He raised a hand to mop his brow. And stopped it midway.

He looked at the gauntlet. Gore fell away.

All dead?

The silence and the stillness were worse than the clamor of the Disaster siren. O'Flynn watched the blood which was already congealing on the gray mesh of his arms, on the grotesquely reddened boots, and now on some junior executive officer's desk. Revulsion flooded through him. He had murdered from rage and panic; now all were gone.

O'Flynn bent to look at the junior's face. Some nerve gas, he guessed. There had always been rumors about Base, this as well as the other big ones. When he had completed his second year of training, a temporary instructor had told half the class of the secret anti-personnel weapons held in case of emergencies. And the powers invested in the Base controller. The instructor was gone the next day, his place taken by a cheerful explosives expert who would not have believed in the scene O'Flynn now contemplated even if he had been present. O'Flynn found difficulty in accepting what had been done: to ensure the death of one man, hundreds had been wiped out. And if he had completed the gesture of wiping sweat from his forehead, if he had not been stopped by the sight of the blackening blood on his gauntlet, he would have taken off his helmet and joined the still flaccid corpses ranged around him.

He pushed himself away from the desk, trod carefully around the dead men, and went deeper into the neat corridors.

"O'Flynn is dead," the robot informed him. "Do not enter Base for one hour. The air is contaminated by an accidental discharge. Repeat. All crews outside Base remain with machines at main lock for one hour."

It was beginning to repeat the message for the benefit of the crusher crews as O'Flynn entered the innermost recess of the vast interstellar vessel.

There was nothing there. The room was bare, bleak and brightly lit. No robot figure; no mass of circuits; no series of elegantly finished housings. Almost nothing: a small cone of hazy light on a wall. Base Controller—a shimmer of energy waves. He could destroy it with one blow.

"You," said O'Flynn.

"O'Flynn," agreed the robot. "Crush the ship," it added. "All crushers. Destroy Base. I say again, destroy Base."

"Could they?"

"They will."

It was a confrontation from nightmare. Cold, implacable, the thing ordered its own certain destruction. O'Flynn began to move toward the silent cone.

He had nothing else to say.

The crushers began to grind at the sides of the ship.

"Base Control relinquishing command," came from the room, from the helmet, from the cone. It was a confession of suicide.

The ship lurched.

"So this is how it ends," said O'Flynn.

The years of training; the joy of working with a succession of fine teams; getting his own dead team together! work on a dozen satellites; the moment of idle curiosity when the sliver of rock with its anachronism fell into his field of vision; the useless killings. Ended.

"No."

From the room, another voice. Then a different one.
"No. I agree. I wish to see this O'Flynn."

A third voice came, querulous and quavering.

"You're out of order. There isn't even a proper motion about it."

"No," agreed the first voice. "There isn't. My decision, however. Base!"

"Base reporting, Base Seven."

"O'Flynn. Bring him."

The cone shimmered excitedly.

"Hurry, O'Flynn. Get into take-off chamber."

"No."

"No?"

It was the first speaker again. From where? O'Flynn had followed the conversation with difficulty. He had forced himself to stop the one blow that would shatter the thing that called itself Base Control; instinct ordered him to live on, no matter for how short a time. But who was the speaker? And the other? *What* were they? And how could they intervene with such authority? Was it someone—something—from the local Sector?

O'Flynn caught himself looking about the bare room for some hint of the nature of the speaker. Smooth walls—nothing else. *From Galactic Center?*

"Why not, O'Flynn?"

"Why?"

"You must know by now. Anything is better than extinction. And you did wonder about the presence of the wretched meter!"

"Yes."

O'Flynn turned. The journey through the still corridors was worse than before.

Chapter 4

Beyond the Galaxy on the still world once called the Forever Planet the bizarre equilibrium held. Infinite density balanced the pressure of infinite gravity. The forces promised chaos, brought terrifying results to a handful of unfortunate voyagers, dragged them into a sink of gravity where matter whistled into being and as rapidly completed its cycle of existence and whirled away into the emptiness of time.

The Timepivot hung to the planet, waiting.

Chapter 5

"No," said O'Flynn when he saw the thing. "No."

A gravity chute had flung him from the vessel. Still dazed from the shock of the clanging journey through the dimensions, O'Flynn had been given no rest, no respite, no assurance that he could plead his case, no warning of the nature of the thing which now regarded him.

"Yes, O'Flynn. I'm a miracle. It's just as well I am, not only for yourself but for the sake of your entire ludicrous race. Though in a way I have to include myself."

Mutant. Aberration. Thing.

It was a mound of flesh. It stretched above O'Flynn so high that he had to crane backward to see the colossal dome which in a human would be a head.

Height: two hundred feet.

"No!" said O'Flynn. "No!"

A mound of flesh two hundred feet high. In roughly the shape of a human figure.

O'Flynn backed away from the gray-pink mass. Layers of fat shook in merriment.

"I don't believe it," said O'Flynn firmly.

"On a point of information," began a new voice. O'Flynn tried to locate the speaker, since the thin piping was not from the top of the thing. "On a point of order, Mr. Charisman. . ."

"No! No!!" screamed O'Flynn. He was at the far limit of sanity and what he now watched brought ancient fears of primordial specters skittering through his mind.

A mouth had opened in the thing's knee. A gaping mouth, with a complement of teeth, lips, tongue and saliva. It was talking.

"Yes?"

The thing was speaking again.

"Well, Mr. Charisman, is this or is this not O'Flynn? And, if I might be so presumptuous as to ask again as a matter of information, precisely what is an O'Flynn?"

"Jesus," said O'Flynn.

"Jesus?" said the mouth. "Jesus?"

"An O'Flynn's part of the Plutarch cycle," said the mouth. "A Jesus I don't have data on."

"Jesus," said O'Flynn again.

"Jesus O'Flynn?" said the mouth on the knee.

"Fill him full of sand!"

O'Flynn stumbled backward. Another mouth had opened on the mountain. It was a small, pursed mouth immediately opposite him; it opened from a toe.

"You'll both resume silence or I'll do just that," promised Mr. Charisman. "Don't you find them tedious, Jesus O'Flynn?"

O'Flynn realized that, far from his having suffered an hallucination, the thing was still before him, talking sanely and somewhat confidentially.

"You," he tried to say. It came out as a strangulated gasp.

"Me. Go on."

A mutant, O'Flynn was telling himself, an accident of genes, a thing that was the misbegotten progeny of some fearful pair of humans, themselves links in a chain of gene transmission through a series of radiation and viral transitions that had resulted in Mr. Charisman. *Mr. Charisman!*

"Do collect yourself, O'Flynn. I'd like to throw the meeting open to my colleagues; you've seen two of them already, by the way. Take time, but not too much. It's what I—we—find ourselves short of."

"You—" began O'Flynn. "Real?"

"Clearly."

"Me?"

"Why? Yes." Mr. Charisman considered O'Flynn from protruberant eyes. "Listen carefully O'Flynn. I am Mr. Charisman. The Ruler of the Galaxy. Someone's got to do it; not that I wouldn't resign if I got half a chance . . ."

There was an interruption. Three more mouths opened, to say almost in unison, "Hear! Hear, hear!"

". . . wants a stop!" Another mouth made itself heard above the din. "Time must have a stop!"

It was a large mouth. In the opalescent light, O'Flynn distinctly saw a flash of metal and a trickling of sand down the coils of fat.

"I do apologize," said Mr. Charisman. "You'll hear about that before long. If we let you live."

"What chance have I got?"

O'Flynn heard his own words, and he marveled at himself. Unseen attendant robots had stripped him during the winging trek through the storms of hyperspace; he had been fed, his body had been exercised, his mind rested. And now he faced something that commanded the unit he had labored for; commanded more than that, much more.

"We'll go into that when I throw the meeting open. For the moment, listen. Now, as you've gathered, I'm a miracle. I shall live for another two hundred and twenty-two years, two hundred and twenty-two days and about eighty-seven seconds. You, on the other hand, have a possible life span of fifty years. But you've almost wrecked my plan for the Galaxy! You can't understand the danger you represented when you found that wretched instrument. Standing Orders for any discoveries of this sort provide for the deletion of all humans in contact with the discoverer. Do you follow this, O'Flynn?"

"I think so."

"Come closer. I can see we're going to be friends."

O'Flynn said "Jesus!" once more as a chute flipped him upward. He was staring into eyes—into one eye—the size of boulders.

"That's better, O'Flynn," Mr. Charisman murmured. "Let me tell you about Operation Plutarch."

The mouth curved in a gentle, reminiscent smile while O'Flynn's concept of existence shredded away.

Chapter 6

Operation Plutarch, so the nightmare mutant told O'Flynn, was a manifestation of the Pyramid Syndrome. The trouble with the human race, Mr. Charisman said, was too much leisure allied with too much technological capacity. Hence, some inspired Nilotic has made the extraordinary conceptual leap and devised a system of combining the two. Surplus leisure could be utilized in a technological *tour de force*.

"And so the pyramids," said the thing. "A beautiful conception: the pursuit of an eternal monument through eternal endeavor. The pyramid ethos joined all sectors of society in one solemn and utterly useless undertaking. There was nothing quite like it until the early days of space technology."

Mr. Charisman explained. The first space probes had sent men to Old Terra's long-dead satellite, Luna. Back had come the precious cargo: two buckets of pulverized ash. And so it had gone on, until wholly unremarkable samples of rock and dust had accumulated on Old Terra, brought at immense expense in terms of human endeavor from the entire Solar System.

"Once committed to the exploration of the system, there was no end to the process; at least, not for some centuries. As each team of designers produced more sophisticated deep-space vessels, so there was a call, chiefly from the designers, to maintain the team in existence. The pyramid builders had shown the way. Higher and more complex pyramids, faster and bigger vessels, until the warp shift was understood and the stars were investigated."

There was an end to exploration, O'Flynn learned. The story fascinated him; it stirred half-remembered ideas the youths of his class had once dared to whisper

24

about the days of Old Terra, the feats of the early hyperspace travelers, and, once and once only, the legend of the travelers who ventured beyond the rim of the Galaxy itself. Mr. Charisman told of the end to exploration. There was nothing left to find out in the Galaxy. And attempts to cross the gulfs beyond had led to Disasters.

"Of course, there was no particular problem of overleisure during the centuries of exploration," said the gross mouth. "You'll readily understand, Jesus O'Flynn, that, what with the Frames—you don't know about those? no matter—and with the labor needed to keep pushing back the frontier, there was enough *occupation* for the entire human race. And then there was the occasional war, of course. That helped."

"I, my team, Base—it was never at the rim of the Galaxy," O'Flynn said. He had accepted everything the monster told him.

"No! How clever!"

"Blasting the mountains—it was a method of using surplus technological capacity."

"Yes! Well done, Jesus O'Flynn! We may be able to make use of you. I may be able to throw the meeting open to my colleagues soon. You will accept a little more information, won't you? I feel you're hovering on the brink of insight, but you could guess *wrong.*"

"You control the Galaxy."

He regarded the mass with awe.

"I invented Operation Plutarch. It came to me when I investigated the reconstruction of the old Solar System. After Blow-up, a replica of Terra was made. And Luna, of course. A harmless piece of nostalgia, to produce an artificial earth and moon; charming piece of period reconstruction."

O'Flynn began to understand what a pitiable thing the human race had become, ruled by this mountain of flesh which passed its time inventing occupations for its members.

"I extended the idea—adding an ancient philospher's curious conception of the nature of the moon's configuration."

"Yes," said O'Flynn. "One team reduces a satellite to smoothness, polishes it . . ."

"And along comes the reconstruction team to raise the mountains and gouge the valleys! Don't you like it?"

O'Flynn understood at last.

There was nothing to strive for. Everything he had been trained to do was a sickening parody of action. He, dead Karanja, poor slow Lingelbach, deluded Preston, the men who had perished at Base—all had been living through a corporeal fantasy; all had suffered the delusion of energetic and noble involvement with a fine cause. Nothing had been real.

Only this gargantuan caricature of a human being was real.

He, O'Flynn, had ground away at the surface of a score of planets—or was it the same planet each time? —and then other teams of dedicated and inspired engineers and landscape designers had faced the hard, polished, compacted, mirror-like moon and clothed it with a mantle of natural features.

"A beautiful cycle," breathed Mr. Charisman. "You know, Plutarch thought that Old Luna's surface was a shining mirror. He said its 'seas' and 'mountains' were reflections of Terra's own configuration. What a charming idea! And what an inspiration it proved to me!"

"And that's all there is?"

"No, O'Flynn! We haven't begun yet! You'll have to do much bettter than that if you want me to propose a motion allowing you to go on living!"

Propose a motion. O'Flynn hunted for an explanation.

None came, so he said desperately, "I found the thermal calibrator; the reconstruction team dropped it."

"That's better."

"They used some plastic process to make the rock."

"Good!"

"And when I found it, the operation was endangered."

"*Very* good, O'Flynn. It's quite remarkable, the way you've adapted. You're a bit of a phenomenon, you

26

know, O'Flynn. Not like myself, of course. I'm a miracle. Did you know the probability figure for miracles, by the way? No matter, I'm running into my colleagues' time. I'll tell you later, if you survive their questioning. But you are a bit of a rarity, O'Flynn. I hope you're going to help me with my little problem."

"Problem? You!"

"Don't be surprised. It's a personal matter." The mouth hung slackly for a moment in a fearful parody of sadness.

O'Flynn shook with relief when he saw it. Now that he believed that the mutant, the aberration, the colossal bulk of the thing that called itself Mr. Charisman was real, he could begin to hope. It had a use for him.

"You've done quite well up to now. I had an encouraging report from that obsessive Base Controller you had. The trouble with these robots in that they're so *inflexible!* Quite useless for my problem. You did quite well. Yes. A useful idea to keep your suit on once you'd penetrated Base. What made you do it?"

"It didn't occur to me to take it off."

"Your movements would have been less impeded."

"Yes."

"So it was instinct. Better still. You'll find a good set of instinctive responses useful where you're going; if I can convince my colleagues you're the one we want, that is."

O'Flynn felt curiosity stirring in him. He had no doubt that Mr. Charisman could destroy him without interest or compunction if he wished; but he also began to realize that the thing was interested in his potential as a tool.

"How could I help?"

The eyes focused on O'Flynn's still shaking body.

"It's a matter of time, Jesus O'Flynn. Time."

"Time?"

"A piece of time."

O'Flynn listened as the mystery began to take on a shape.

Chapter 7

Mr. Charisman's explanation demolished what little was left of O'Flynn's old life. He began to understand what he was to do.

It was, as the impossible grotesque said, a matter of time.

Once, in a remote past, some daring voyagers had set out across the Universe to find Time itself.

They had found it.

Timepiece.

The plain, factual account of the Timepiece expedition had not attempted a complete description of the strange fusion of forces which hurled the Forever Planet's architects back into their own universe. There was nothing in it to suggest that in the anomalous math of that furious equation there was a frozen *junction* of time. But legend has seized on the story and embellished it, sometimes with a gross absurdity, sometimes with uncanny artistic insight.

No factual account or ornate legend could adequately describe the terrifying reality; nothing more than touched on the awesome existence of the complex of hypercubes, the localized creation of a universe in thermodynamic equilibrium which only a few chanced to see. None returned, though a mutinous gang of condemned criminals—brains keyed to the main computer banks as a safeguard; a failure, since the computers themselves were warped by the fantastic gravitational forces exerted by the planet—did send news of their impending disastrous crash as their captured vessel whirled off into the vortex of forces surrounding the planet's many dimensions. Their story passed into unholy legend too: the ride of the dead men into the gaping pits of hyperspace.

Undead, they lived in the memory of the storytellers; and perhaps they had an existence too in one of the broken continua left behind by the planet's original designers. Perhaps they, like the incredible Suzanne Rosetti, swam through a succession of microstates, each generating a new microstate, each a unique and specific model, each one a link in the chain of timelessness which was the legacy of the creatures who had built the planetary workshop.

Chapter 8

Mouths opened.

The quivering enormity became alive with a hundred voices, each yelling for attention.

"Order!" groaned the vast, central mouth in the great head. "I will have an orderly meeting!" it roared, deafening O'Flynn, whose whole body clamored for peace as the vibrations set up by the multimouthed thing made his brain quiver in its shaking skull.

"I must have a motion first! I will not, I cannot proceed with the business of this meeting unless I have a motion on the floor!" Mr. Charisman smiled at O'Flynn. "Playful, that's what they are. Playful."

"You are a . . ."

"Miracle, O'Flynn. Do you want proof?"

"No!"

"It's your life. If you can convince the meeting, that is."

"Convince us!" screamed a mouth, a thin purple-lipped, jelly-like mouth that grew from Mr. Charisman's nose. It closed abruptly as the shimmering mechanism which had filled one unfortunate mouth full of sand began to move gently in its direction.

"On a point of information," said a gash in Mr. Charisman's chest.

"Yes?"

"Is O'Flynn *able* to help us? Has he the necessary understanding of our problem?"

"Hear!" called a score of mouths. "Point of information!" added another. "Answer!"

"No," said Mr. Charisman. "Not yet. Have you, O'Flynn?"

"I'm beginning to understand," lied O'Flynn. Confidence. The unforced, brisk answer. He hoped he would begin to find the parameters of comprehension before long; discussing the unknown with this unthinkable grotesque was not altogether without interest. For all his horror and unbelief, O'Flynn found his sense of curiosity increasing. "I believe I can help," he lied again.

"You've heard O'Flynn," said Mr. Charisman.

"Point of information!" squealed a mouth from Mr. Charisman's right foot. It grew from a tuft of green hair so that to O'Flynn, two hundred feet above the mouth, it seemed that the voice came from a clump of vegetation.

"Yes?"

"Can't we simply *stop* everything? I mean, do we have to trouble ourselves with things like Jesus O'Flynn up there? If I might go on, Mr. Charisman, aren't we a visionary, hierarchical and authoritarian committee, with unlimited powers? Can't we just stop time?"

"No," said Mr. Charisman. "Speak again and it's sand for you." In an aside, "Don't pay any attention," Mr. Charisman said to O'Flynn. "He's simply anti-human."

There was a babble of protest from some of the mouths. O'Flynn heard phrases like "Disgraceful!" "Simply prejudging the issue!" "Undemocratic!" and "Blah-blah-blah-blah!" from one grinning mouth on a fat forearm.

"Perhaps we'd better not have a formal motion," said Mr. Charisman. "I'll take a straw vote on whether or not we go into general discussion of our problem. Who says 'Aye'?"

"Aye!!" roared around O'Flynn, setting up shock waves through the whole of his body. He jerked epileptically within the soft web which held him aloft and facing the mutant Mr. Charisman. Two low-pitched voices attempted "No!" but they were ignored.

"Very well," said Mr. Charisman. "The business of the meeting is suspended. We'll talk about the reorganization of the Frames on a date to be decided. The trouble with the outer systems on the Schine radials will keep too. Go on, O'Flynn."

O'Flynn watched mouths quiver expectantly. Mr. Charisman expected him to speak.

"On a point of information," said O'Flynn in desperation. The mouths turned down slightly. Mr. Charisman frowned.

"Go on," it said at last.

"I must know exactly what you wish me to do."

"Tell him!" squealed half a dozen mouths.

"Certainly not!" said Mr. Charisman. "How could he help us stop if we told him what to do?"

The crazed illogicality unbalanced O'Flynn. He shouted. "Try me! I'm O'Flynn, the murderer! I killed a whole Base full of my friends! I can do anything!"

"How clever, O'Flynn," said a small voice admiringly. O'Flynn looked for its location, but he could not find it.

"May I speak, Mr. Charisman?"

It was an important-sounding voice. O'Flynn looked down and saw that a chasm had appeared in the enormous gut below.

"Do," said Mr. Charisman. "Do, please!"

"It's obvious to me," the mouth began, "that in this rather delicate situation we have to look exceptionally at the exceptional."

"How wise!" said several mouths. "How right!"

It went on, unperturbed.

"We have to look at the *desirability* of letting a complete and utter buffoon like O'Flynn—and he is, you know, quite a *clown*," it said to laughter, "we have to ask ourselves whether we wish to disturb the prevailing conditions. I mean, is it *proper* to ask an O'Flynn, however talented in turning up the unexpected, to act as agent on our behalf? After all, we have been Lords of the Galaxy for two hundred and twenty-two years, not to mention the days, hours, minutes and seconds of our ascendancy over mere humans, and we shall continue to direct the destinies of the stellar systems of the Galaxy for another two hundred and twenty-two years, not to mention the odd days, hours, minutes and seconds . . ."

"If you could get to the point," Mr. Charisman suggested. "I think O'Flynn's flagging. If we're to use him, it would be better not to wear him up. Fragile things, these humans." No voice could have sounded less concerned.

"If you think so," the mouth in the navel said with composure. "Shall I merely say, do we wish an O'Flynn to find the Timepivot?"

Timepivot.

O'Flynn knew.

He could endure this meeting—*meeting?*—this entry into a horrifying, grotesquely enduring and sustained nightmare assembly of mouths.

"No!" squealed the mouth in the green growth far below. "Swallow him! Ingest him!"

"Give big mouth down there a treat!" bellowed a vicious mouth full of long fangs which O'Flynn had not seen before, and which had suddenly opened in Mr. Charisman's shoulder.

"Order!"

Mr. Charisman moved, at which the sanding machinery edged menacingly toward the shoulder. The mouth disappeared. Nevertheless O'Flynn lapsed momentarily into shock-induced unconsciousness.

Timepivot. It was his waking thought. He realized that his fainting fit had not been noticed.

"I can't stomach him," a sweetly reasonable voice was complaining. "He's a reactionary."

"Who is?" asked O'Flynn.

"You're joining the debate, O'Flynn?" said Mr. Charisman. "How pleasant!"

The voice larded with reasonableness came from Mr. Charisman's naked crotch. O'Flynn looked down. There was no sign of sexual parts. Folds of fat encased what in a human would be the navel. The voice went on.

"Good to hear from you, O'Flynn! I said I can't stomach—belly—big-mouth gut. I've never been able to stand him since the miracle that's us began over two hundred years ago . . ."

"I said I'm a miracle," said Mr. Charisman, sounding pleased at that factual acknowlegment.

33

"Yes, I can see it," said O'Flynn. "You want me to help find the Timepivot."

"O'Flynn!" said the reasonable voice. "O'Flynn!"

"Jesus O'Flynn," pointed out several mouths.

"Jesus O'Flynn, then! I believe we can go on to a formal motion! Can't we, Mr. Charisman?"

"Can we?" called Mr. Charisman. "Straw vote."

It was passed. None of the dissenters queried the procedure. O'Flynn, learning the rules for this ghoulish encounter, knew that some of the members were with him; the thing that ran the Galaxy would formally debate his continued existence. In its own service.

"Propose, then," said Mr. Charisman.

A new voice interrupted. O'Flynn saw that it came from the top of the great dome, bald and shining wet with perspiration, which surmounted the colossal head.

"I think my silence has been my principal contribution for the past two hundred and twenty-two years, two hundred and twenty-two days, two hundred and twenty-two minutes . . ."

"Where are you?" bellowed Mr. Charisman irritably, and appealed to O'Flynn. "I didn't know we had him! Where is he?"

O'Flynn pointed out the mouth's location.

". . . seconds," went on the dull voice, "But now I feel I have to speak. I've never opened my mouth before," it went on wonderingly.

"Then speak!" said Mr. Charisman.

There was silence.

"Speak!" said Mr. Charisman again. "If anyone has the right to say something, it's you! I know I'm out of order, but I make the rules! That right, O'Flynn?"

"You make the rules," said O'Flynn.

There was silence. The mouth had closed.

"May I go on?" asked the lucid and sweetly reasonable voice from the navel. O'Flynn looked down and saw that he was wrong. There were sexual parts. The voice had come from an opening on the flank of an enormous testicle. A slight shifting of Mr. Charisman's bulk as it tried to look at the top of its own dome had revealed the reasonable mouth's exact location.

"I think that's all from him," growled Mr. Charisman. "Go on, please."

"Yes. Very well. I shall. Good. You listening, O'Flynn? Jesus O'Flynn?"

"Yes," called O'Flynn. "Yes, sir," he added.

"How polite! Well, now that our colleague has decided to continue to preserve his stupendous silence, I feel one of us should attempt a résumé for O'Flynn. Then a formal proposition. Is that in order, Mr. Charisman?"

"Very well. Yes." Mr. Charisman grinned in a friendly fashion at O'Flynn. "I make the rules."

"Well, for O'Flynn's benefit—Jesus O'Flynn's, that is—I'll simply say that we, collectively, are a little *tired* of it all. We're not irresponsible. We just want a vacation."

"You've not had one for two hundred and twenty-two years," said O'Flynn in a moment of inspiration.

"Not to mention the odd days," said the testicular mouth.

"Get on with it," said Mr. Charisman.

"We've all accepted in principle that the situation of this committee must be changed, Mr. Charisman. Therefore, I move formally that Jesus O'Flynn be delegated to change it."

"Seconded!" screamed a high-pitched voice, again one which was hidden from O'Flynn.

"Buttock butting in," said the mouth in the great gut.

"He needles me," said a mouth on a kneecap.

"He's in order," said Mr. Charisman. "I now have a formal proposition, duly seconded." To O'Flynn he said, "You're going to make it, O'Flynn. I do believe you're to be delegated."

"To find the Timepivot," said O'Flynn.

Not only was he learning the rules of this multi-mouthed horror's methods of procedure, he was beginning to realize precisely what was required of him. In some way, by upsetting the delicate balance of purposeless creation and then destruction of planetary mantles, he had proved that he was capable of intuitive action; presumably this grotesque which claimed that it ran the

35

Galaxy was incapable of such action. And, again presumed O'Flynn, the thing either couldn't or wouldn't find another human being to undertake the quest for whatever it sought.

"I don't trust O'Flynn, however," added the reasonable voice from the enormous testicle. "Put a ring in his nose."

"Yes," said Mr. Charisman. "A little bomb in his belly. To keep you alert and attentive," he told O'Flynn. "It won't hurt."

"How long shall we give him?"

The speaker was the hidden mouth, high-pitched and clearly unpopular, which had seconded the proposal to send O'Flynn on the unknown quest.

"We haven't voted on the proposal yet," said Mr. Charisman. "We'll vote now."

"I move an amendment."

Daring Mr. Charisman's threat to fill it with sand, the voice was that of the antihuman mouth on the green-clad foot far below O'Flynn. He could see the corners edged down in a malicious smirk.

"I move that we delete O'Flynn!"

Mr. Charisman hesitated. Looking down, the ponderous head inclined forward, so that the cliff of a nose almost touched O'Flynn. A gigantic hair, curling from the nasal orifice, threatened to impale him. He wriggled aside, retching in fear, cold with fatigue and still slightly amnesic from the horror of the encounter.

The face retreated.

"You're out of order. I make the rules."

"But Mr. Char—aaaaaargh—ugh-ugh-u. . ."

O'Flynn watched sand cascading into the spiteful mouth.

"That should keep him quiet for a year or two," said Mr. Charisman with quiet satisfaction. "Now we'll vote. Every mouth shall speak. And it shall say 'Aye.' "

"Aye!!!" came from mouths which opened on hands, under folds of fat and previously hidden from O'Flynn, "Aye!!!" shrilled from armpits, from great pits forming momentarily in the gigantic pectorals, from tiny rosebuds lost in the recesses of Mr. Charisman's ears.

"Aye!!!" echoed from mouths filled with great black stumps of teeth, from mouths blistering the fetid air with a horrid halitosis, from mouths in some stage or other of infant development and which contained only pink new gums, or one incipient fang; from mouths primly chopping the single syllable off with one sharp "Aye," and from wide-open mouths bellowing loud and long in uproarious approval; from sycophantic murmuring mouths which smiled "Aye," and from surly mouths which snapped an "Aye" through tight-clenched teeth, clashing enormous fangs in the general direction of an almost insane O'Flynn.

"I'll have to adjourn the meeting," said Mr. Charisman. "The poor fellow's so overwhelmed by the honor you do him that he's fainted clean away."

Chapter 9

Locked in a radial of continua, still keyed to the imprisoning circuits of the computer systems surviving, the criminals from a score of interstellar centers blindly attempted to contrive some meaning from their predicament; a sense of *being* was still theirs. But in the freak conditions of the Forever Planet, for them there was no *now* or *when* or *here*. They pivoted slowly about a fixed cycloid, living through a brief series of events, the same events, again, again, and again.

There was evolution even within the cycloid.

Through the continued working of the computers to which their minds were linked by tendrils of impulse-emitters, they began to attain a group consciousness. As yet there was no direction for it.

There was nowhere to go, nothing to do.

Their feeling of purpose remained dormant.

Chapter 10

"How are you, Jesus O'Flynn?"

O'Flynn groaned when he saw the thin purple jelly-lipped mouth before him. He had dreamed it all; this was his conclusion. There was no thing with mouths, no enormous horror as big as an interstellar vessel, no Mr. Charisman filling mutinous mouths with sand and ruling the Galaxy. In his dream, Karanja was talking.

"It's an untouched moon, O'Flynn! Look at it! Those peaks—how are we going to shift them?" And O'Flynn had told Karanja how the team would set about the task; the new fission materials someone at Base had worked on would provide the most spectacular blasting operation ever. "We'll do it, O'Flynn— you're a minor miracle, O'Flynn! You're the best ever!"

"Sure I can do it!" he groaned to the poor corpse.

"Well, good for you, O'Flynn!" boomed a cavern before O'Flynn's unfocused eyes. "You'd better, we've put a little bomb in your belly. Now we're going to put a time limit on you!"

O'Flynn's hands sought his tautening belly. The muscles writhed away from a newness, a strange feeling of metallic menace, He found it. Small, almost insignificant. Deeply embedded into the muscle wall of his abdomen. His control.

Mouths clamored for Mr. Charisman's attention.

"I wonder if I might be allowed to interject a point here . . ."

"Blah-blah-blah-blah . . ."

"It's my recollection that O'Flynn expressed a certain anxiety ab . . ."

"This isn't a formal proposition, it's more in the nature of a suggestion for proceeding in this iss . . ."

39

"I love your ideas, belly, but here we have . . ."

"Quiet!"

Mr. Charisman obtained silence. "A comment from each who has a positive contribution. *Positive,* I said."

"Alert the Hunters," said the malicious purple lips.

"We don't know where they are," said a hidden voice.

"We've no formal contacts with them," said Mr. Charisman.

"Hunters?" asked O'Flynn.

"You'll find them," promised Mr. Charisman.

"Alert them," agreed kneecap. "Make it a race."

"Put a time limit on O'Flynn," melodiously suggested the chasm in Mr. Charisman's navel.

"Let's make it a race!" said the reasonable testicular mouth.

"Give him how long?" asked Mr. Charisman when the cheering which greeted this suggestion had died down.

"We can't give him unlimited time," said a petulant voice. O'Flynn could not see where it came from.

"With respect, Mr. Charisman?" asked the cavern in the belly.

"Yes?"

"Why not give him some of our time?"

"How long?"

"Part of our remaining two hundred and twenty-two years, two hundred and twenty-two days, two hundred . . ."

"Not years," said the mouth on the nose. "He'd be dead."

"We can't give you two hundred and twenty-two years, can we, O'Flynn?" asked Mr. Charisman.

O'Flynn wondered if he would begin to laugh hysterically if he spoke; it was all true, he told himself, every ghastly moment of it. Now the thing was asking his advice. Dare he suggest that he be given a time limit of two hundred and twenty-two years?

"You make the rules, Mr. Charisman," he said diplomatically.

"So I do," agreed the thing. "So I do."

"Is this supposed to be a democratic comm—" began a voice which followed the line of warts on Mr. Charisman's left ear. It tailed off and said no more.

"Why not give Jesus O'Flynn say, say, two hundred and twenty-two say, say—" O'Flynn began to hope "—seconds!"

There were murmurs of approval. "No," breathed O'Flynn.

"Yes," said Mr. Charisman. "Get the Timepivot. Start on my countdown. From ten. No. Start now."

"In less than four minutes!" screamed O'Flynn. "It can't be done!"

"Why not?" asked Mr. Charisman. The mouth formed into a great and amused pit. Mr. Charisman began to guffaw.

"Human beings can accomplish most things in four minutes," pointed out the pleasant and melodious mouth from Mr. Charisman's gut. "Why not you, O'Flynn?"

"Yes. Start now."

O'Flynn was on the crystalline floor. Before him swam the towers of New Terra, though as yet he did not recognize it as such. He made no move.

"They can grill a steak—grill four steaks," said a malicious mouth.

"Write a sonnet," said a soft rosebud.

"Wind up a debate," called another.

"Run a mile!"

"Procreate!"

"O'Flynn wouldn't know how!"

"Ho-ho-ho-ho-ho-ho-ho-ho!!" roared Mr. Charisman. A warm rain filled the air above O'Flynn; he dodged enormous drops. Mr. Charisman was crying with laughter.

"You've failed!" one of the mouths shouted. "You've had your time, O'Flynn!"

"Let me have him!" bawled a mouth immediately above O'Flynn. "I've never had one before!" Sharp teeth clashed cannibalistically. "Please, Mr. Charisman!"

"No!" squealed O'Flynn.

"Yes!" boomed Mr. Charisman.

"You said I should fetch the Timepivot!" shrieked O'Flynn. He could already feel the vile breath of the hungry mouths.

"You failed, O'Flynn!"

"On a point of information, Mr. Charisman!"

The thing, the grotesque, the zany, inconsequential, monumental, horrifying mound was still; its mouths hung open expectantly.

"Point of information?"

How mad was it? Would it abide by its own crazed procedures?

"I have a question," O'Flynn gasped.

"Go on."

"What did—" O'Flynn paused in almost breathless desperation. What could he say? How could he halt the thing and turn its attention away from its obvious purpose of extracting as much entertainment as it could from his predicament before it put an end to him? "What did the clockmaker say to the old grandfather clock?"

Grandfather clock? What had made him say it? Who, where, how had he heard of things like *clockmaker* and *grandfather clock?*

"I like a riddle," said Mr. Charisman. "Well?"

"You have to answer," said O'Flynn. "You have to try."

His mind reeled. In what way could he turn the thing's mad arguments against itself?

" 'What are you so wound up about?' " guessed the mouth in Mr. Charisman's navel.

" 'Who rang your chimes?' " said the mouth on the kneecap.

"Good!" said Mr. Charisman. "That right, O'Flynn?"

"No."

Time. It was a matter of time. The whole of this surreal encounter was about time. O'Flynn tried to float himself off into another space and time where Mr. Charisman could not find him.

42

" 'I like your swing.' " suggested the cannibalistic mouth immediately above O'Flynn.

" 'You've got a cheek!' " giggled the voice on the testicle nervously.

" 'You're an unbalanced old thing,' " said a bored voice.

The mouths closed firmly. Mr. Charisman said, "How about that, O'Flynn?"

"No." Memories flooded into his mind. A flood of confidence washed away his fear and horror. He could confront the thing and brazen a way out of this absurd situation. He said, " 'You're a silly old Timepiece.' "

"That's not funny," said Mr. Charisman. "It's not even as funny as 'I like your swing!' "

"It's funnier," said O'Flynn. "It's funnier than your suggesting I find the Timepivot—and the Hunters—in four minutes."

"Are you sure?" asked Mr. Charisman.

"Certain."

"We'll take a vote," said the thing.

And, in the vast crystalline cavern in which the thing lived out its span of four hundred and forty-two years, four hundred and forty-two days, four hundred and forty-two minutes and precisely four hundred and forty-two seconds, a vote was taken. The ruler of the Galaxy counted the votes for and against O'Flynn's continued existence.

And if I do survive? O'Flynn, whose phantasmogorical experience now made him think of himself as Jesus O'Flynn, let his mind play on his immediate future. He knew now what he was; he guessed where he might be; he had an inkling as to what Mr. Charisman required of him; and he knew with cold certainty that the metallic weight in his belly might rip him into scorched carrion at the thing's whim.

Most of the mouths said "Aye." A few mumbled incoherently. One or two refused to open. O'Flynn was aware that only the monstrous grotesque's vote had any significance.

Hunters? Wondered O'Flynn. *Hunters!* The word

had dropped into his mind when he had not been able to do more than combat his terror. *Hunters?* And *Timepivot.* They were linked, O'Flynn decided.

"Passed unanimously, O'Flynn!" called Mr. Charisman. "That means we all agreed! You're to have, Jesus O'Flynn, two hundred and twenty-two hours! You start when you've had your training."

"Jesus!" sobbed O'Flynn. "What am I to *do?*"

"That's your problem," said Mr. Charisman. Soothingly he added, "You have my committee's fullest confidence, O'Flynn."

"That's the way, Jesus O'Flynn," said a voice. It came from Mr. Charisman's left testicle. "I really think you should make the best use of your time."

O'Flynn walked to the gravity chute.

It coiled toward him and hefted his almost paralyzed body into the sparkling and circuitous windings of a vast city's transport system.

The last thing that O'Flynn saw of Mr. Charisman was the glum, closed mouth of the cannibalistically inclined member of the swag-bellied nightmare's committee.

Trainers?

Chapter 11

"Catch, O'Flynn!"

Power roared through O'Flynn's drooping body. He caught the sword by the hilt in one lightning movement. Then he fought for his life.

There were two of them, one a woman. *A woman!* O'Flynn had no time to inquire into this extraordinary turn of events, for they were on him. Two needle points advanced in deadly, flickering circles, seeking the easy, barely resisting vital spot in throat or belly; two lithe figures behind the points could scarcely contain their joy.

"Mr. Charisman's sent us another!" whimpered the man.

"It's an O'Flynn!" the woman said.

They were almost identical; black-clad in tight-fitting one-piece garments; old, thin, with long flat muscles ridged blackly: experts.

O'Flynn lunged experimentally at the woman. She caught the sword strongly, tried the strength of his wrist and held him rigid as her twin grinned.

"You didn't get past the first session," giggled the man. The point moved slowly toward O'Flynn's throat. The man was enjoying himself. Spittle drooled from his mouth, down the aged, lined face and onto the thin chest. "Keep him there, Jessica darling!"

"You weren't the one," said the old woman. Jessica. "Mr. Charisman was quite, quite wro . . ."

O'Flynn disengaged, slashed wildly at the advancing point, threw the sword, javelin-fashion, at the woman's bony body, and ran. He was in a gymnasium. Rows of weapons; mats; energy suits; ropes; shields; a ringed space for free-gravity fighting; realistic dummies

45

nodding in the slight breeze; dull-faced fighting robots —but no obvious way out!

The woman began to scream. O'Flynn took in the scene at a glance. The sword she had flung him was now embedded in her bowels; the man had both hands to a vast gash running down one side of his gaunt red-splashed face.

"Bravo!" called a voice.

O'Flynn looked for it. "Splendid! A master stroke!" *Where was it coming from?*

"Hurry, O'Flynn—it's a puzzle!"

The floor began to shake.

A line of robots began to advance across the scarred floor of the gynmasium. *A puzzle?*

He had been thrown a weapon by—by the Trainers, O'Flynn decided. This was training? Blood? Violent death? They—it—something had given him a weapon to defend himself against the two gaunt experts who were supporting one another as they gouted blood at the other end of the gynasium. Where was the weapon?

Ponderously the robots laid massive tracked feet on the quivering ground. A weapon against *these!*

Above the sullen grinding of the tracks, O'Flynn could hear the dying woman squealing. There must be a weapon! Rows of spears. Against fighting robots? Energy suits which floated contestants high above the ground and emitted their own force-fields, to be used when a man was least expecting it in one single bolt of pure energy. There was not time to get into one! What he needed was a fission weapon—whose blast would kill him too!

O'Flynn raced for the line of training robots.

"Good, O'Flynn! You made it by about three seconds."

A single control panel directed them. Years of experience with a thousand different types of bearer-robots had accustomed O'Flynn to handling the ponderous machines. *Attack* read one control. *Fusion* another. *War Alert*. O'Flynn set the robots in motion.

"I don't think we'll trouble with the outcome, Jesus

O'Flynn," said the voice. "Come along. Down the free-grav ring."

The two lines of robots locked. Gobbets of fire rolled from end to end of the line. The enormously heavy tracks of one robot fragmented the equipment, the racks of archaic weapons, the suits. The robot trainers hesitated at the writhing bodies—and then moved over them.

The rest of the contest was lost to O'Flynn's gaze as the free-gravity arena shot him upward and through the high dome above.

"Not bad, O'Flynn,'" he was assured. "Not bad at all."

A gnome. A deformed creature. One possessed of a huge pair of forearms and a mane of yellow hair.

"I came for training," said O'Flynn.

"So you did. So you did. Well, train away, that's what I say."

"Swords? Swords?" O'Flynn saw that he was in a room whose stone walls were hung with the gnome's trophies. The perfectly preserved heads of men who had clearly failed in their training courses.

"They have their uses, O'Flynn! Have you ever considered the sheer functional beauty of the hand weapon? Look at it!"

Steel. An ancient weapon, cross-hilted, straight, single-edged, diamond-pointed.

"I've never used one before."

"And you needn't learn now—you didn't come here to learn to be a swordsman, O'Flynn! Mr. Charisman has plenty of flashing heroes on call. Trained by me, naturally," said the gnome.

"Tell me what I have to do," said O'Flynn.

"Now that, O'Flynn, is what you have to decide."

"Jesus!" said O'Flynn. He was almost strong enough to feel angry.

"Jesus O'Flynn then, if it'll make you feel better," the gnome said complacently.

It didn't.

He had expected a well-defined program, some sort of preparation to face—face *what*?

47

"Hunters," said O'Flynn. "Mr. Charisman said the Hunters."

"Never heard of them," assured the gnome. "What are they? Some new sort of sect? There was a pack of beasts in the Vegan System who had to be put down. Called themselves Searchers. No—Seekers. Very nasty tricks they had, took almost the entire Galactic Fleet to contain them, once they'd got their heads." He pointed to the trophies. "Brought one back with me for training my people. Not much stamina. You were better, O'Flynn; pity you can't join my team here."

"And what's that for?"

The gnome waved a hand around the room, which now appeared much bigger than before. "We clean up," he said briefly. "Mr. Charisman trusts me. Thought he'd made a mistake when he sent you along, but you did well, O'Flynn. Nice idea that, using Jessica as a dartboard. She'd have died laughing if anyone had told her she'd get hers like that. You're a vicious bastard, O'Flynn."

"Why the reception?" O'Flynn asked.

He knew the answer already. There was no pattern whatsoever in Mr. Charisman's disposal of him; he was being given a short period of grace before his two hundred and twenty-two hours began to tick away. His belly contracted against the metallic weight of the bomb.

"Just the usual sort of thing, O'Flynn. I'd have called Jessica and Wilfred off if you'd been in any real danger. Maybe."

"And the training? When do I start?"

The gnome grinned at him and dug him sharply in the ribs; O'Flynn chopped down savagely on the gnome's thick shoulder.

"Playful, O'Flynn. Mr. Charisman said you were." The gnome rubbed at the shoulder for a moment and then said, "What sort of training do you want?"

Jesus! O'Flynn groaned inwardly. Another jovial maniac! First the dreadful monstrosity which said it ran the Galaxy and now this mini-grotesque who was to train him; for what, neither of them knew.

48

"I was to find the Timepivot," said O'Flynn.

The gnome shot upward, as if propelled by an energy beam. Its twisted face registered acute interest and extreme excitement.

"That's what you're after, is it, Jesus O'Flynn? You'll need some preparation for a venture after the Timepivot!"

Chapter 12

Centuries ground away. Time flowed about the warped gravitational fields of the Forever Planet, surging up and washing over the weird matrix of forevers left behind by the makers of the planetary workshop.

The drift of time did nothing to the trapped criminal brains riveted to the still active computer banks. But there was a kind of evolution even within the cycloids. A growing awareness of identity began to accumulate, grain by grain. A sense of oneness with the succession of microstates radiating from the core of energy left behind when the masters of the planet swam away into their own universe.

Chapter 13

"Meet the team," said the gnome. He pressed a bright-red button and the walls fell away. O'Flynn wished he had not, for a refinement of distilled horror was revealed. "Mr. Charisman's idea again," said the gnome proudly. "He gave me these to bring into line."

The team floated in separate baths.

"Have you eaten lately?" inquired the gnome, with an accession of hospitality. O'Flynn groaned. "Our friends here—my gaggle of intellectuals. Don't let them worry you. They've been dead for centuries."

It was the stench of the long-dead. The sweet-sourness of corruption, the arrested decay of organs, the interrupted disintegration of bones. In coffin-like tanks, bodies bobbed and eddied as air bubbles cleansed whatever ghastly liquid it was that sustained a measure of activity in the ghouls. For activity there was. Eyes turned whenever a head rolled to face sideways; eyes promised retribution should they gain the power they had lost; gray-white hands gripped fetally drawn-up knees, hugging hatred, terror and unattainable vengeance.

"Call me Gilfillan," said the gnome. "Gilfillan's here, messmates!" he yelled around the enormous laboratory. "Who's going to volunteer to help this time?"

O'Flynn retched and heaved, holding to a table for support.

"Not there, O'Flynn!" called the gnome, seeing where his hand lay. "Mr. Charisman had an old gentleman from the Third Millennium dug up a couple of days ago, and all that's left of him is spread out where your hand is."

"Ughhhhhoooooah!"

51

"You *are* in a state of nerves, Jesus. Try some of this."

O'Flynn allowed himself to be led away from the remains to an alcove. He scrubbed his hands and found the gnome Gilfillan proffering a glass. He drank it in one gulp; it was poor, lost Karanja's remedy, a drink whose preparation had come down through the ruin of the old worlds. "More!"

"Not too much, now! There's someone you've got to talk to."

"One of these?" whispered O'Flynn.

"A survivor from the original expedition," the gnome said. "He was given a Galactic Hero's funeral —all the trimmings. Nervous system suspended, pumped full of that foul stuff they found in the Debrix ghost ship that had passed out of the Galaxy and come back without anyone aboard. Big honor that, O'Flynn. You might get some of it if you survive. I won't." Gilfillan regarded his charnel house. "Not sure I'd want it. Come on, O'Flynn. Time for your first fill-in session. After that, we might get the old boy to suggest some training program or other for you."

O'Flynn allowed himself to be led back into the laboratory; nothing could be worse than what he had seen. *Could it?* He had believed that there could be no more ghastly sight, for instance, than the cannibalistic mouth high up on Mr. Charisman, or the malicious purple-lipped mouth on the thing's nose. He had assured himself that no sensation could be more horrifying than that of murdering Preston, then Karanja and Lingelbach. But hadn't the first sickening realization of the end of his state of innocence been worse than these? Was there really a refining of ghastliness, or had he become a different O'Flynn, an O'Flynn overlaid by calluses of terror and stark pity?

The gnome was watching him.

"You'll do, O'Flynn. Come and see Henry Sokutu."

"Henry Sokutu?"

"One of the team—the survivor of the Forever Planet expedition I was telling you about. Hero's funeral and all that. Nice old boy, as they go." He raised his voice to a ringing falsetto. "Hare! Burke! My assistants," he explained.

Two robots trundled forward. There was nothing in any way different from any other servant robot; until O'Flynn noticed that each was crowned with a piece of headgear, black, circular, with a black disc of the same somber material at the base. It emphasized their gaunt frames; the black, surely ceremonial headpiece, O'Flynn guessed, was some joke of the gnome's. Gilfillan offered no explanation. He was humming to himself as the two robots busied themselves about one of the baths.

"He's clever," said Gilfillan. "Tricky too. You can't trust these revived boyos, O'Flynn. Some of them don't mind being reactivated, but most of them hate it. Claim it's an intrusion of their personal liberty, though how they square that up with what really happens, I don't know. Man, they're dead!"

"How long has this one been dead?"

"Centuries. Mr. Charisman isn't sure. There was a time when the records got obscured. Three, four centuries maybe."

"And they can be brought back to life?"

"No. Reactivated. We can run impulses through their nervous systems if they're in good enough shape, and those that got the Heroes' funeral are. Here, they're ready."

The head was encased in a shimmering haze of coagulated energy bands. Protection, guessed O'Flynn. The body bobbed slightly in the tank. Bulbous eyes stared ahead without movement, almost without expression.

"Give him the full shots, Hare," said Gilfillan. "We want him for about ten minutes. Can't overuse them," he explained. "Burns them out. Now, Professor," bellowed the gnome, "I'd like you to meet my friend Jesus O'Flynn!"

"No—one—has—a—name—" creaked the reconstructed voice, "like Jes—Je—Jesu—Jesus O'Flynn!"

"A humorist," said the gnome. "Stir him up a bit," he told the attendant undertaker robot.

"Sir," said the robot mournfully.

A trickle of radiant light entered the liquid where the corpse which talked swam. *Was this the worst?* O'Flynn asked himself if this torturing of the dead was more horrible than anything else.

The voice creaked out; "I was Professor Sokutu—I hear you—Gilfillan!"

"He was a great joker," said Gilfillan. "I almost don't like doing this to him. Tell O'Flynn here about the planet," he ordered. "Tell him what he needs to know to understand what happens there."

"Is that all? Only that?"

The voice was stronger through the unmoving lips, the artificial vocal apparatus working better now that Sokutu's dead mental circuits were responding more willingly; alert for the trickiness Gilfillan had warned of, O'Flynn noted the hint of irony. He ignored it.

"I have to visit the planet. What must I know?"

Henry Sokutu, or what remained of him, let out a distorted wheeze; it could have been the reconstruction of a laugh.

"It's a hole in the universe—a bolthole! Don't go through it, Jesus O'Flynn!"

"What did you leave behind?"

"Ghosts, O'Flynn! Ghosts in the gravitational maze; you won't find them, however hard you look. They ripped the Key from Garvin's mind, and they went back to their own place, O'Flynn."

"The Timepivot. There's something you called the Timepivot."

"I called it that? I must have done. I must have had a reason, O'Flynn. What was it?"

"I want to know."

"The golden flower—the mandala, O'Flynn—that's what I left behind. I should have gone into it myself!"

"Should I go into it?"

"You won't find it! There's just the ashes of the Key's structure left—only the ruins of the engine! You won't find the Key to time, O'Flynn! Only the thing you can pivot time on—if you can find how!"

The robot undertaker murmured to Gilfillan.

O'Flynn was trying to take in the data, to store in each word, allowing it to filter through the store of information he had gleaned from the thing which controlled the Galaxy.

"Make it easy for me," he begged.

"They manufactured hyperspace," said Henry Sokutu. "They built a gravitational engine which controlled the fabric of their immediate part of the universe!" There was a degree of awe in the artificial voice, faithfully reflecting the traces of emotion remaining in the corpse's memory circuits, translating preserved chemical and electrical tenuousities into Sokutu's known speech patterns.

"Who did this, Sokutu? Who made the engine? Why did they leave anything behind?"

Both robots were conferring with Gilfillan. The gnome appeared indecisive, but O'Flynn barely noted his reactions to the undertakers' concern.

"Why, the . . ."

"Overloaded!" reported Hare. "Too much, sir!"

"He's going," said Gilfillan. "I'm in trouble!"

Long-dead Sokutu's eyes glowed once and then emptied. A genuine, if centuries-delayed death rattle bubbled from the twice-dead corpse.

"He can't devise your training schedule, O'Flynn," said the gnome. He was contemplating the putrescent corpse as if willing it into a third existence. "He was the only one in the team who could do it for you! Physicists we're stocked to here with! Field theorists we have a surplus of. We haven't another polymath, though! He was the greatest of his kind, so Mr. Charisman said. Tricky! Sometimes I thought he could put one over Mr. Charisman himself."

Stupidly, O'Flynn said, "But he was dead."

"I was never sure," said the gnome. "I'm glad he's gone."

"And me."

They both meant it. They left the undertaker robots to dispose of the remains of Henry Sokutu.

Chapter 14

The planet still surged with life. Its sexagesimal pattern of gravitational cores remained potent, stored with matter dredged from imploding white dwarf stars of minute mass and almost infinite gravity. Fantastic forces struggled within each minute core. The six glowing cores interlocked, heaving time and space into freak dimensional chains. And, abandoned by its makers, what was left of the dimensional engine exerted a random control over the chains of forces.

At some stage, the wreck of the prison ship which had ferried the criminals to the remotest part of the Galaxy, and which endlessly toured one cycloid of existence, came into a brief conjunction with the other ruin; the remains of the engine which had controlled the Forever Planet. The Timepivot.

A pattern of identification was completed in that brief conjunction. The remaining computers automatically registered its presence, assessed its powers, and guessed at its purpose. Their brains locked to the computers, the prisoners absorbed the information.

They developed a purpose.

Chapter 15

"I have to find out about time," said O'Flynn.

"How do you work out a training schedule for that?" said Gilfillan. Much of the humor and all of the aggression had left him; the removal of the remains of Henry Sokutu had been an unpleasant experience to supervise. He had little to offer in the way of advice. Clearly he expected trouble from his master.

"What *is* time?"

Gilfillan left. "Use the Thinktank," he suggested as he went. "Compliments of the establishment."

Still curious about the establishment—O'Flynn had worked out that it was Mr. Charisman's own creation, for training his devious emissaries in whatever unpleasantness had to be done about the Galaxy—O'Flynn decided to extend his stay as long as possible. He found food, he slept, and then he took stock of his position.

It was not an enviable one. O'Flynn could draw back from his predicament and see at once that he had survived so far by a combination of luck and superb reflexes; he could assess himself to some extent too. It was obvious that he belonged to a tiny minority of the human race; he was among the number who were channeled by Mr. Charisman's organization into apparently elite battalions. He had been indoctrinated from his earliest youth into a willing acceptance of his future as a member of Operation Plutarch, that grim joke of the two-hundred-foot mass of flesh that ruled the Galaxy. And yet he had been able to adapt to a new set of circumstances. He had been able, for instance, to make the first rebellious move of refusing to accept Base's urgent injunction to cut himself off from contact with the team. Unsuspected powers of decision and determination, allied to great physical strength, had enabled him to defeat the robot controller of the Base Mission. But what, O'Flynn asked himself, had sustained him through his ghastly encounter with Mr. Charisman? And with long-dead Sokutu? Something like confidence strengthened O'Flynn's thoughts. Though he was to be given a ludicrous time limit for Mr. Charisman's quest, he knew that he could call on reserves of intuition and qualities of adaptation which were phenomenal. Perhaps he, like Mr. Charisman, was something of a miracle.

The immediate problem was to prepare himself for the search for the Timepivot. *Time. Pivoting* time? It had to have meaning. O'Flynn called for one of Gilfillan's robots.

"The Thinktank. Explain."

"Yes, sir." Was it one of the attendant pair Gilfillan had called Hare and Burke? No matter; robots of this grade were from the same mold, their small idiosyncracies developing only through their observation of an owner's patterns of life. This one was cautious with apprentice agents, as Gilfillan had been. Without haste but without reluctance, the dull-faced robot explained.

"It's a feedback, sir. Information feedback. You pose an idea and you get a run of information to supplement it. It's more than a container of information though, sir. It speculates."

"It's not linked to those?"

O'Flynn gestured to the stone walls beyond which lay the bobbing cadavers.

"Oh no, sir! The Thinktank is entirely robotic!"

"Set it up."

"I have already taken that liberty, sir."

O'Flynn confronted the Thinktank. There was little in its conventional layout to suggest a special ability: the usual comprehensive body container with its firm cushion of air; the searching needles which would connect the nerve endings in his hands to its controls; O'Flynn had used such machines in his own training days. He found himself smiling for the first time since his discovery of the embedded meter. It was a new beginning, with an altogether more hazardous career ahead.

"Time," he said to the machine. "What *is* time?"

Chapter 16

"Time," murmured the machine. "Time is the unusual dimension."

"How?"

"Time is the unusual dimension because it is calculated or described or structured subjectively. It is the interval between events. Without events, there is no time."

"Go on."

"Time is an *a priori* representation. Try thinking of an absence of time. Try it."

"A time empty of time?"

"A dimension called time in which there is an absence of time. It's not a new idea."

O'Flynn let the idea possess him.

"No."

"The human mind cannot conceive the time dimension empty of events. It can record the incidence of events and compare the intervals of time between them, but it cannot conceive of a time empty of time. It can measure the intervals at which an electron spins, or the rotation of a planetary axis, or the temporal progress of a stellar system. For the human mind, space and time cannot be separated."

"Can you think of time without time?"

"Not me," said the machine. "But I can tell you who might."

"Tell me," said O'Flynn.

"You asked first about the unusual qualities of time. Those first?"

"All right."

"Time is irreversible. Time appears in an unusually symmetrical way. And yet time is elastic."

"Elastic?"

"It isn't difficult to devise another description of time. In one well-known cosmology, time isn't a time-invariant thing. Time lengthens with time. Old things age quicker; new things slower. There's no such thing as a constant factor in the aging of the structure of the universe. Any two observers at two different points would see two different time dimensions," the machine murmured.

O'Flynn wrenched himself from the implausible metaphysics into which it launched; as he listened to the arguments, he became more and more certain that it was not this pretentious construction which would help him. He tried once more.

"What are the Hunters?"

"They're the ones I told you about."

O'Flynn tried to make the adjustment, but he could not find the common factor.

"Explain."

"You asked if anyone could think of a state where time did not exist—where there was no way of measuring the interval between events."

"And what is it?"

"The Hunters know it. They exist in a closed continuum where the ordinary symmetry of time does not apply."

"And what are they doing there?"

The machine allowed itself a philosophical chuckle.

"Now that, Jesus O'Flynn, is what Mr. Charisman is concerned about."

It refused to discuss the details of the Hunters' purpose, characteristics or existence. Try as he might, O'Flynn was not able to divert the flow of speculation about the human mind and the nature of spatiotemporal relationships. He learned that space and time are not general concepts—without understanding what a general concept was—but merely intuitions; he heard an erudite discussion, with the machine taking both sides of an argument, concerning the impossibility of movement in a nontemporal world, and how a succession of equilibrium states might or might not move in a given direction.

The machine chuckled disagreeably when he tried to interrupt; it came to O'Flynn that Mr. Charisman was determined to make things difficult for him.

"O'Flynn!" yelled Gilfillan, when his mind reeled from argument and counterargument. "You've had all the training you're going to get! Mr. Charisman wants you out of here. Pity you can't meet the rest of the team, but there it is, life isn't all Totex and tits around here, more's the pity—wahh!" bellowed the long-haired gnome. "Wah-wah-wha! I was forgetting—you're not interested in that sort of thing!"

"What sort of thing!"

"You'll never know, O'Flynn!"

O'Flynn regarded the muscular gnome uneasily; whenever a portion of the female anatomy was mentioned, he found himself edging away, as if from contact with unknown and taboo evil.

"I have to go? Isn't there anything else you can put me on to, Gilfillan?"

Gilfillan grinned. "I shouldn't help you. Orders. But look for the Timepeacers, O'Flynn; you'll get more than one surprise there!"

O'Flynn began to be afraid of the unknown. He began to hear again the obscene roaring of the mouths on Mr. Charisman's mountainous body; he remembered the sickening dissolution of Henry Sokutu, and a mortal terror destroyed his brief accession of confidence.

Chapter 17

"Consider that," said a voice. O'Flynn looked up. Normality. A paunchy, distinguished man, conventionally clothed, unwashed, and genuinely concerned at O'Flynn's distress. "I haven't seen a man blubbing in daylight before. No, sir. Not in my fifty years of New Terra. You've given me hope, whoever you are. Wouldn't like to say, would you?"

"Jesus O'Flynn."

"*Jesus* O'Flynn?"

"Me."

"What did they do to you, Jesus O'Flynn? Quite a name that, boy! Mine's Hillock."

"How are you?"

"More to the point, how are *you?*"

"I wish I knew."

"You been in the Frames? Got lost—that it?"

"Not that."

"In the Globes? Can't find your way back?"

"Not that either."

"Sick?"

"No."

"Then how come you lie there, flat out in the middle of the boulevard? The sweeps could just make a mistake, you know."

"The sweeps?"

"Sweep you up just as if you were stark dead! I've seen it happen; couple of times. Someone stretches out, maybe a good old-fashioned sleep without any bugs or drugs, then whish! and away he goes into the disintegrator! Keeps the place tidy; couldn't do with stinking deaders all over the place, but it's a nasty way to go if you don't want to! Why blub anyway?"

O'Flynn contemplated murder.

He had remained in a catatonic trance for two whole hours, waiting sickly for the hammering of the voices to die down in his battered skull. Still they bawled, hissed, groaned and roared at him. *Timepivot. Hunters. Time!* And now this amiable philanthropist was interested in him.

"Go away," he said quietly.

"Me?"

"You. Now."

"I'm your friend! I could be a friend of a blubber with a name like Jesus O'Flynn!"

"You have to, don't you see," said O'Flynn. "Because if you say one more word, my head's going to split wide open and then I'll wring your fat neck until I've screwed your head off!"

The man backed away. He appeared about to say something. O'Flynn's hollow face and searing eyes stopped him. Nevertheless he took a small disc from his pocket and flicked it to O'Flynn.

He left and O'Flynn automatically put the identity disc in his pocket. He hadn't looked at it.

In another hour he could begin to look around and take in the everyday life of the biggest city in the Galaxy, New London. He had been ejected into a municipal garden where few came. Now he shook himself from the trance which had gripped him and rose wearily to his feet.

The total absence of noise was delicious. The garden was an enclosed oasis with its own weather dome; outside, the raucous life of the city beat against an invisible force-barrier. O'Flynn had seen a city before, but nothing like this. It puzzled him that Mr. Charisman had set him down on this re-creation of an antique world. Why? O'Flynn regarded one street of colored buildings down which a ritual flagellation was in progress; a couple of hundred people, men and women, with a few older children, were capering naked, the more athletic turning handsprings, each with a snaky whip, each lashing out at his nearer neighbors. They were shaking with pain and laughter. O'Flynn turned away; it was a harmless enough pastime. Like shining lunar landscapes into brilliance. A score of tactile crocodiles marched zanily through another street; in each crocodile, perhaps three hundred people kept up a rhythmic step, each person joined at head, hip and knee to a neighbor. O'Flynn dimly recalled having heard of the craze for togetherness which had culminated in the physical attachment—permanent, with bone welds—of person to person in one long, amicable chain. *Mr. Charisman's idea?* Was this another of the thing's notions for keeping the human race happy? O'Flynn shrugged. It was no more his problem than that of the silver-clad, diaphanous-winged, wand-bearing and fragile-boned men and women who hovered over the soaring buildings like so many gorgeous insects; no more O'Flynn's problem than that of the huge-breasted women—women? O'Flynn paused but his curiosity was not sustained—who dwelt on polystyrene clouds above New London, served by self-abased worshippers who lived in dread of immolation at the command of the goddesses they adored. Then O'Flynn saw the petrified people; anchored in golden tubs, they gazed unwinkingly ahead at every street intersection. They were the ones who had opted for total immobility; Mr. Charisman had devised a technology for maintaining life without the least physical movement. *Did they still think? See?*

"It's not my problem," said O'Flynn aloud.

He tried his legs. The shaking had lessened.

He walked out into the streets.

You're as ready as we can make you, Jesus O'Flynn, Gilfillan had said. *Now go out and see what you can do.*

"Now," O'Flynn asked himself, "now where do I start?"

Two hundred and twenty-two hours, less those he had spent recovering from the shock of being pitched out into a world he had only heard of: New Terra, center of the Galaxy, the infinitely desired capital of the settled worlds, the *manufactured* planet, whose configuration followed as closely as loving care could make it the planet from which the conquest of the

65

Galaxy had begun. Where, on this world of human chains and frozen men and women in golden bowls, was he to begin to find a way to a planet which existed only in the folk memories of a people and in a few reports surviving from the old Federation?

"Please get off my head," a voice said.

O'Flynn leapt three feet into the air. He had been standing on a troglodyte; he looked again and saw that a nest of the interred men and women were stirring in the loose gravel he had walked on.

"No more!" O'Flynn said shakily. He hurried to a quiet street away from the chanting trains of humans who, conjoined by bone grafts, marched rhythmically past its entrance; none spared a glance for him. Each pair of eyes was fixed on the head in front.

"Like to join a witch hunt, darling?" whispered a voice in his ear. O'Flynn cowered away from a fresh young face hovering above his left ear; the apparation carried a vicious-looking trident. "The Baal crowd are getting uppity. Come and join the fun! We could use a pair of shoulders like yours!" It whistled piercingly and a pair of similarly diaphanous-winged youngish men floated down, to hover above O'Flynn.

"I really haven't the time," said O'Flynn, gazing in fascination at the nine loosely held and glittering points.

"*You're* not a hocus-pocus joker, are you?"

The fresh young face smiled in anticipation.

"You wouldn't be a thaumaturge thickie, would you?"

"We hate them," explained the third.

"No!"

What mad ritual had he now stumbled across? O'Flynn knew without the need for close analysis that the three beribboned, gossamer-winged harpies would be delighted to sink their tridents into his cringing flesh.

"I'm looking for the Hunters."

There was a new note in the noise of the hovering wings; powerful motors surged; the three were moving away, O'Flynn saw with relief.

"Wouldn't be you!" called one of them.

"Sons of Belial!" whooped another.

O'Flynn ran for a doorway. Then he saw that the three were not interested in him; a troop of large, gowned, staring-eyed and beared men were winging across the rooftops toward the trident-bearers. Screams and roars filled the air.

"Lean somewhere else, there's a dear," said a voice from the doorway. "It's feeding time for my babies." O'Flynn leapt away from the enormous, opalescent buttocks against which he had placed a palm; a woman was suckling something that had two heads and a shimmering tail.

He ran out into the sunshine and ricocheted off a pair of potted humans, who ignored him absolutely. A pattering of footsteps lent power to his legs; turning, he saw that a girl riding a tiger was chasing him.

"Wait!" she called sweetly. "Wait for me!"

O'Flynn reached for the sword Gilfillan had insisted he take; it rasped out for half its length. Then he pitched head over heels as a pair of hands reached from the hard ground below his feet and gripped his ankles. The yellow eyes moved closer.

Chapter 18

"You must be from out of this world," the girl called.

O'Flynn edged a hand toward the hilt of the sword.

"Don't do that! Thanks, Troggo! Keep calm—he'll get excited if you go for a weapon. Still, Waldo!" The girl was at home in this strange place. The troglodyte which had brought O'Flynn down grunted and slid beneath the ground once more; the tiger sniffed delicately at O'Flynn's outstretched hands. "It's all right!" she said. "I'm on your side, O'Flynn. Waldo smelt you out by the disc."

"Can I move?" asked O'Flynn, who was fighting a fearsome cramp in his shoulder. *Disc?*

"Yes. Slow, though. Waldo!" the girl warned.

O'Flynn looked down the smooth line of her belly to the blonde pubic hair where it merged with the bright stripes of the tiger's fur. He swallowed, still apprehensive of the beast; following the girl's instructions, he got to his feet without haste, keeping his hand from the steel hilt.

"We haven't got much time," the girl said. "There's a Civil Liberties Night tonight. Starts soon. That's why the trogs are keeping their heads down. The fairies started their fun early. I hope they're cut up! But you, poor thing! What a mess you're in! Walk beside Waldo; you can put your hand on his collar. It gives him a bit of reassurance." The girl followed O'Flynn's gaze to her delicate pink nipples. "I thought you Moonshiners were desexed at birth."

"Please," said O'Flynn. "Please let me get away from here. I have things to do."

"Yes. Oh, you poor, poor thing—*man!* You don't know what the time of day is here, do you? Hillock said you'd be lost. But never mind, O'Flynn, we'll soon

68

get to the Sindrome. Come on." She jerked her heels into the tiger's belly. It growled at O'Flynn, a subdued surging noise. The girl reached out and put his hand on its collar; the hand trembled uncontrollably, but the tiger appeared mollified.

"The Sindrome?" asked O'Flynn. He could have added *Civil Liberties Night? Hillock?* and *trogs* and *fairies,* not to mention the semitransparent woman who was feeding—*what?* He remembered the casually flung disc. It had served to identify him.

"It's not far, O'Flynn. You must be in a frightful haze about all this. What with all that moonshining and then meeting our Glorious Leader!"

"Mr. Charisman," said O'Flynn. "You can't mean Mr. Charisman!" The girl couldn't speak disrespectfully and in those ironic tones of the ruler of the Galaxy.

"Hypostatic Hrungnir himself," said the girl. "I expect he gave you a bad time. Come on!" she called suddenly. "No patience, some of these trolls!"

The dying sunlight was itself overcast by a cloud of leather-winged creatures, stark-black and hideous.

"Run!" shrieked the girl. "No! Not him!" she howled to the tiger, as it turned enormous fangs toward O'Flynn. "Those!"

Ahead, blocking their progress, was a pair of gaunt women. Each was equipped with a brace of saw-edged knives.

Chapter 19

Grain by grain, the purpose became a rocklike resolve. *The Timepivot was their heritage!*

There was no understanding on the part of the trapped brains, no true comprehension, no formal decision. Locked in their endless succession of unique microstates, the condemned and shackled brains formed a joint pattern of resolution as the slowing down of fission processes changed a hot and bright star to a dull-red globe. The group consciousness of the slow, tortured minds produced a dull awareness of function. *The Timepivot could provide their personal Nirvana.*

The workshops of the wrecked prison ship still functioned, maintaining what was left of the vessel in perfect working order. The equipment which sustained life in the condemned was, however, barely adequate to its task. Banks of computers considered the problem.

Their solution was to build new life-supporting shells for the trapped brains.

loose stones in the niche rattled and the earth dweller was gone.

"Could you hang on to Waldo's collar while we make a run for it?" asked the girl. She gripped his hand and let it rest against the silken hairs of her navel. "You could use that sword of yours too; all the horribles are afraid of Waldo. I don't think they'd touch me, or Hillock would let the other girls come out with their pets. It wouldn't help you much though. Are you any good with it?" Her eyes sparkled with delight. Whatever their chances of survival, whatever dangers they might come across, here was a creature who lived for the thrill of overprivileged, manic New Terra and its viciously decadent way of life.

A yelping of high-pitched voices alerted man and woman and beast. O'Flynn slipped the sword from its sheath in one swift movement; the girl's smile became a wild laugh; the tiger put its head back and shook the passage with an answering challenge. The girl jumped astride its ridged back.

"We can't be caught here!" the girl called above the banshee wail of the hunting cacademons. "Come on, O'Flynn, hold on and give them the point!"

Out into the gloom leapt the tiger as it responded to the girl's hefty kick; O'Flynn almost lost his balance as he was dragged along. The girl whooped twice and the race was on.

O'Flynn blinked in disbelief as the tiger bellowed its anger and the girl shrilled her delight. But a crackle of wings under acute stress jerked him into the only too physical reality of this latest insane predicament. The girl suddenly yanked the tiger's mane and hauled it onto a fresh tack. "Behind you!" she shrieked.

Needle points scored a triple path across his shoulder, reminding him that the harpies were out in force.

"Pinked him, Anthony!" fluted a voice in O'Flynn's ear.

"Stick him in the rump, Jimmie!" called another. "Don't touch the bawd. Just get the stranger!"

"Will do!" fluted the trident-bearer happily. O'Flynn forced his tiring legs into a stronger rhythm. It was not enough; the light of a hundred moons had begun to illuminate the streets. Pain forced O'Flynn to grind his teeth.

"The point, O'Flynn!" called the girl. "Get him before he sticks you. You can't afford to lose more blood!"

The screaming diaphanous-gowned harpy fluttered down again; by the silver rays of a moon he might have helped polish to crystal brilliance, O'Flynn could see the even white teeth of the effeminate and blood-crazed pursuer. The white teeth and the three needle points of the trident which was bearing down on him, couched against the creature's thin shoulder. Without conscious volition, O'Flynn leapt to meet it.

"Anthony!" shrilled the creature. "Anth—" Its call was cut off abruptly as the sword sheered through chest, power unit and still fluttering wings.

"Come on!" yelled the girl, circling on the tiger's back and hauling O'Flynn away from the harpy he had plucked from the air. O'Flynn tugged his sword free, hefted the vicious trident in his other hand and passed it to the girl. She tossed it out into the street. "Against the rules, O'Flynn; couldn't be found with one of these. Oh, come on—run! Not much further. Look, the old bastard's sent some of the other girls! About time too!" They had reached their destination.

O'Flynn thought at first that he was suffering from an hallucination, that the girl and the loping creature she sat astride were multiplied in his mind through some self-deceiving mechanism he had invented. Six—eight—ten—fifteen—sixteen naked women, bosoms shining and jiggling in the moonshine, bestriding sixteen huge, glowering tigers, were advancing to meet them. O'Flynn learned in that moment what laughter was. Sick with fear and relief from fear, stark terror and escape from the terrors of the demon-infested gloom; stumbling from exhaustion and loss of blood from the deep triple incisions in his shoulder; aware that the naked women were advancing toward him with no

74